Henry and the Something New

By Jenn Bailey

Illustrated by Mika Song

chronicle books · san francisco

To Kevin, who is always up for dinosaur sprinkles.

—J. B.

To my father, who loves dinosaurs.

—M. S.

Contents

Chapter 1
Field Trip Day 1

Chapter 2
The Rules 11

Chapter 3
The Museum 19

Chapter 4
Dinosaurs 31

Chapter 5
Lost and Found 43

Chapter 1
Field Trip Day

Today was Field Trip Day.

Henry was excited.

Everyone in Classroom Ten would ride

the bus to the museum.

Henry was also worried.

Everyone in Classroom Ten would ride

the bus to the museum.

Mrs. Tanaka said, "If you are going on the field trip, please bring your permission slip up to my desk."

Henry found his permission slip in his backpack. If he left it there, he could go to the library.

The library had beanbag chairs. It had a

hamster in a cage.

It also had books! Henry loved books.

Riley brought up her slip.

Katie brought up her slip.

Samuel made his fly like a rocket!

"Land it right there," said Mrs. Tanaka.

If Henry did bring up his slip, he could go
to the museum.

Mrs. Tanaka said the museum had rocks

from the moon. It had real live mummies

that were dead!

It also had dinosaurs! Henry loved

dinosaurs.

Henry handed his slip to Mrs. Tanaka.

"On my desk, please," said Mrs. Tanaka.

"But if a wind comes by," said Henry, "or
a Samuel, it might fall off your desk. It
might get lost."

"It will be safe," said Mrs. Tanaka.

"My mommy is a field trip helper," said

Vivianne. "She says we can see the

butterflies first."

"I want to see the dinosaurs," said Henry.

"The museum is very big," said Vivianne.

"It might be hard to find them."

"Dinosaurs are very big," said Henry. "I

think it will be hard *not* to find them."

Chapter 2
The Rules

Classroom Ten walked down the hall and out the school doors.

Mrs. Tanaka said, "Here are the rules for visiting the museum.

"Rule Number One: Stay with your field
  trip helper. We do not want you to get lost.

"Rule Number Two: Come back to the bus
  at three o'clock. We do not want to leave
  you behind.

"Rule Number Three . . ."

But Henry did not hear Rule Number

Three. A huge bus drove up to the curb. It

was very loud. It rumbled. It shook. It was

so close to Henry that Henry shook, too.

Henry said, "Mrs. Tanaka. Maybe I am supposed to go to the library today."

"You are supposed to go to the museum today," said Mrs. Tanaka. "Please find your seat on the bus."

Henry had not ridden the bus before. He
climbed up the tall steps. He looked down
the long row. Most of Classroom Ten
waited behind Henry.

"Go on," said Jayden.

"Mrs. Tanaka said to find *my* seat," said Henry.

"Just pick one," said Jayden.

Katie waved at Henry from the third row.

Henry always sat next to Katie. At Art.

At Lunch. Even on the swings.

"There is my seat," said Henry.

Chapter 3
The Museum

At the museum, Mrs. Tanaka put them

in groups. Henry would not see butterflies

with Vivianne.

But he would see Samuel. And

Samuel's dad.

Samuel's dad said, "Sorry I am late.
I got lost."

Helpers could get lost? Henry would have
to be extra careful. He did not want to get
lost before they found the dinosaurs.

The museum felt cold. It echoed.

"What should we see first?" asked

Samuel's dad.

"Moon rocks!" said Samuel.

"Bugs!" said Riley.

"Dinosaurs!" said Henry. But he forgot to

say it out loud.

"Rocks and bugs," said Samuel's dad.

"This way."

The Rock Room was full of rocks. Little

rocks and big rocks. Pretty rocks and dull

rocks. Some rocks looked like glass or

candy. Some rocks looked like rocks.

"Those are from the moon," said Samuel.

"There are space suits!" said Riley. "Let's

put them on and hunt for rocks."

"Space is very dark," said Henry. "Someone

might need to hunt for us."

The Bug Zoo was full of bugs. Little bugs and big bugs. Real bugs and fake bugs. Some bugs looked like sticks or leaves. Some bugs looked like bugs.

"This bug has 30 legs!" said Riley.

"A beehive!" said Samuel. "Let's go in and
search for the queen."

"T. Rex is the king of the dinosaurs," said
Henry. "Let's go search for the king."

"What should we see next?" asked

Samuel's dad.

Henry opened his mouth, but . . .

"Mummies!" said Riley and Samuel.

"Mummies!" said Samuel's dad. "This way."

The Mummy Tomb was full of tomb things. Word pictures and clay pots. Baskets and jewelry. And . . .

"Mummies!" said Riley and Samuel and Samuel's dad.

"We can wrap ourselves up," said Riley.

"You can be a mummy, Daddy," said

Samuel.

"Who wants to go first?" asked
Samuel's dad.

Henry sighed. Would they ever see the
dinosaurs?

Chapter 4
Dinosaurs

"What should we see next?" asked

Samuel's dad.

"DINOSAURS!" shouted Henry. He said it

out loud this time.

Samuel had to use the bathroom. Riley had

to get a drink. Henry had to not get angry.

Finally, they saw a sign:

"But which way?" asked Samuel's dad.

No one knew.

They went down one hall and down

another. They turned a corner and . . .

No dinosaurs.

Instead, there was a room behind glass.

Full of machines. Full of people.

Full of bones!

"I think we are lost," said Samuel's dad.

"You might be," said a woman in a white coat. "This is the Bone Room. I am Dr. Seavor. I am a scientist."

She opened the door. "Want to help us find things?"

Samuel and Riley tapped with hammers. Henry brushed away dirt. He brushed and brushed until he saw something smooth. Something that was not dirt.

"A bone!" said Samuel and Riley.

"I would stay here always," said Henry.

"Oh, no," said Samuel's dad. "We can't stay! We need to be on the bus by three o'clock."

"Rule Number Two," said Riley.

"What about the dinosaurs?" asked Henry.

"Dinosaur Hall is far," said Dr. Seavor.

"But we have a secret way."

She led them down a passage. Then she

opened a wide, tall door.

Chapter 5
Lost and Found

Dinosaurs were everywhere!

Little dinosaurs, big dinosaurs, and even

bigger dinosaurs. Some were flying. Some

were swimming. Some were running.

Some looked like bones. Some looked

alive!

Henry closed his eyes and curled his arms around himself. There was a lot of happy to hold inside.

"We found them, Henry!" said Riley.

"With T. Rex right in the middle," said Samuel.

"Thank you, Dr. Seavor," said Samuel's dad.

Henry rocked back and forth a bit. He did

not want any of this happy to slip away.

When Henry got back on the bus, he sat next to Katie. She wore a headband sprinkled with butterflies.

"Everyone followed the rules," said Katie. Her butterflies swayed. "So we get ice cream. You can have vanilla, like always." Henry's happy dimmed. "I might not get ice cream. I might not have followed the rules."

"Did you stay with your helper?" asked Katie.

Henry nodded. "Even when Samuel and Riley went to space."

"Did you get back to the bus by three o'clock?" asked Katie.

Henry nodded. "Even after we stopped for bones. But I did not hear Rule Number Three. Maybe I did not follow it."

"Rule Number Three said to find something new," said Katie. "Did you find something new, Henry?"

"I will think," said Henry.

While he waited for ice cream, Henry thought about rocks floating in space and queen bees hidden in hives.

He thought about brushes finding buried
bones. He thought about a secret door
that led to dinosaurs . . . everywhere!

"Ready to order, Henry?" asked Mrs.

Tanaka. "You look a little lost in thought."

"Sometimes I get lost," said Henry. "But

lost is okay. Lost is where you can find

something new."

It was Henry's turn. He stepped up to the counter and asked for a big scoop of vanilla ice cream.

With sprinkles.

Library of Congress Cataloging-in-Publication Data available.

ISBN 978-1-7972-1390-3

Manufactured in China.

MIX
Paper | Supporting
responsible forestry
FSC™ C008047

Design by Ryan Hayes and Angie Kang.
Typeset in Iowan Old Style.
The illustrations in this book were rendered in watercolor and ink.

10 9 8 7 6 5 4 3 2 1

Chronicle Books LLC
680 Second Street
San Francisco, California 94107

Chronicle Books—we see things differently.
Become part of our community at www.chroniclekids.com.